LION
AND THE
OSTRICH
CHICKS

Books by Ashley Bryan

The Ox of the Wonderful Horns
The Adventures of Aku
Beat the Story Drum, Pum-pum
Walk Together Children
I'm Going to Sing
The Dancing Granny
The Cat's Purr
Lion and the Ostrich Chicks

LION
AND THE
OSTRICH
CHICKS

LION
AND THE
OSTRICH
CHICKS

AND OTHER AFRICAN FOLK TALES

RETOLD AND ILLUSTRATED BY
ASHLEY BRYAN

ALADDIN PAPERBACKS

First Aladdin Paperbacks edition January 1996
Copyright © 1986 by Ashley Bryan

Aladdin Paperbacks
An imprint of Simon & Schuster
Children's Publishing Division
1230 Avenue of the Americas
New York, NY 10020

The Library of Congress has cataloged the hardcover edition as follows:

Bryan, Ashley.
Lion and the ostrich chicks, and other African tales.

SUMMARY: Includes four traditional tales told by the
Hausa, Angolan, Masai, and Bushmen people of Africa.
1. Tales—Africa.   [1. Folklore—Africa]   I. Title.
PZ8.1.B838Li   1986   398.2'096   86-3349
ISBN 0-689-31311-X
ISBN 0-689-80713-9 (Aladdin pbk.)

for
MAUREEN HAYES
with LOVE & THANKS

AFRICAN PROVERB:
If the people of the town and village
are all happy, look for the chief.

CONTENTS

LION AND THE OSTRICH CHICKS

Once upon a time Papa and Mama Ostrich prepared to have a family. Papa Ostrich made a nest in the sand for Mama Ostrich. He swooped about and scooped out a shallow hollow. He smoothed over all the lumps and bumps. Then Mama ostrich stepped in, settled down and laid six eggs.

Mama and Papa Ostrich took turns sitting on the eggs, Mama by day, Papa by night. They warmed the eggs and watched and waited. One morning, six weeks later, six little ostrich chicks kicked their way out of their shells.

The parents circled round their children. They scuffed their two-toed feet in the sand and sang:

"Ostrich stretch, strut, stride and race.
Six little chicks just joined the chase.
Clap for Ostrich, one, two!
Stamp for Lion, shoo, shoo!"

Papa Ostrich boomed out the good news for all to hear. His deep lionlike roar startled the six little chicks. They ran to their Mama.

"Nothing to fear my chicks," said Mama Ostrich, hugging them to her. "That deep, hissing roar is your Papa's voice."

She brought them closer to Papa. The chicks listened as he sounded his deep, hissing roar again.

"That's our Papa," they chirped. "Well, all right, Papa!"

The chicks were so excited, they jumped into the air and fluttered their wings in flight. Down they tumbled to the ground.

"Two pretty little wings," said Mama Ostrich. "But too tiny to fly."

"Now don't you cry," said Papa Ostrich. "We can't fly high on our wings, but we sure can fly on our feet. Watch me!"

Papa Ostrich raced from a nearby bush to a distant tree and back.

"Uh-huh," he said. "Did you see my fleet feet fly? We're the only two-toed birds around, and we use our feet to cover ground."

Papa Ostrich taught the chicks his best running tricks. Every day the chicks practiced their steps: stretch, strut and stride. They got better and better and ran faster and faster.

Weeks passed and soon the chicks could outrun everyone around. They challenged Zebra and Hare and left them in the rear. They raced Deer and Fox and left them in the dust. They were fit and fast and always finished first. Finally they could even keep up with their parents.

"You're fast and that's fine," said Mama Ostrich. "But don't run off too far from home, not until you're fully grown and know your way around."

"We won't," they promised.

Each day the six chicks ran farther away from home, but they remembered their promise. They always turned back before they had gone too far.

One morning the chicks awoke before everyone else. They rose early to practice dashes, relays and sprints. Now that they had learned how to fly on their feet, they didn't miss wings at all.

"Let's go!" they cried.

Away they ran. They raced from their home to a nearby bush. They rushed past the bush to a distant tree. From the tree they chased to the hill beyond. Down the hill they sped, then around a pond. They flew on their feet to a field full of rocks. They leaped and they hopped and came to a stop. They fell on the ground and rolled around. They had run so far. They felt so proud. They laughed and gasped and caught their breath. "Ah . . . Whew! Ah . . . Whew!"

They'd had so much fun running, they hadn't given a thought to where they were going or how far they had gone. They looked around, and they didn't recognize anything.

"Where are we? We're lost! We're lost!" they cried.

Just then a reassuring, roaring sound came from behind the mound of rocks ahead.

"Papa! Mama!" they shouted. "Here we are!"

They ran as one to the mound of rocks and peered behind. Suddenly, shrump! Lion swept all six chicks into his den.

"Welcome home, children," Lion roared.

"You sound like Papa," the chicks said. "But you don't look like Papa at all. You're all fur, four feet and no feathers."

"I can stand on two feet, too, just like you," said Lion. "I'm your papa now."

Lion tapped their stomachs, hmm, and licked his lips, mmm!

"You must be tired, my little chicks," said Lion. "Now go to bed."

When their children didn't come home that day, Mama
and Papa Ostrich searched everywhere until it grew dark.
The chicks were nowhere around, nowhere to be found.

The next morning they set out early to ask if anyone
had seen their chicks.

Everyone said, "No," until Mama Ostrich asked
Mongoose.

"I was up early yesterday," said Mongoose, "and I saw them running. They ran from their home to a nearby bush. Then they ran from the bush to a distant tree. They raced from the tree to the trail up the hill. I saw them running with all their might till they crossed the hill and dropped out of sight. Now just past the hill there's a pond below. If they circled around and didn't fall into the pond, they were bound to come to the mound of rocks—where Lion lives. You don't suppose . . ."

Mama Ostrich's heart went flip-flop. She didn't wait for Mongoose to finish and she didn't stop to think or to thank Mongoose.

She rushed off, whish! past the nearby bush. She raced past the distant tree, whee! She sped on the trail up the hill beyond and she picked up speed as she circled the pond. Then she came to the mound of rocks, whoa! She stopped. Just ahead was Lion's den. Lion sat at the entrance guarding the chicks.

"My children!" Mama Ostrich cried when she saw her chicks.

The chicks hopped up and down.

"Your children? Uh-uh! My children!" said Lion.

"Anyone can see they're mine," said Mama Ostrich.

"Anyone is no one," said Lion. "And you'll need someone to stand up to me."

Mama Ostrich was confused by Lion's crafty talk, but

she wasn't confused about whose children Lion was claiming as his own.

"Stop that Ostrich-hop," Lion said to the chicks. "Do the lion cub crouch I taught you. If you step out of line, snip! I'll snap off your heads. You're lions now. Did you hear what I said?"

"Oh! Don't mistreat them," Mama Ostrich said. "And please don't eat them."

"Uh-uh!" said Lion. "Not now, anyway. But when they're fatter, that will be another matter. Now take off, you tall-necked, long-legged, two-toed, top-heavy bird!"

Lion bared his teeth and growled.

Mama Ostrich fled for help.

She found Papa Ostrich. They went together to tell their story to Chief Counselor Fox and the animal counselors. The counselors listened and agreed to help.

"A strange story, but a simple case," they said. "It's apparent that no true parent could possibly mix cubs and chicks."

"Uh-uh," said Papa Ostrich. "That's Lion's tricks, not Lion's chicks!"

"Oh, look!" said Mama Ostrich. "Here comes Lion now. He's walking my chicks!"

Lion came striding by, walking upright with the six chicks in tow. The counselors bowed politely to Lion.

"Meet my children," Lion said.

"Nice chicks . . . er . . . children you have, Lion," the counselors agreed. "What a fine, feathered family!"

"Uh-huh!" said Chief Counselor Fox. "Note the resemblance."

"Stop him," Mama and Papa Ostrich cried. "Everyone knows those are our children."

But no one dared stop Lion as he walked off with the chicks.

Mama and Papa Ostrich decided to call a meeting of all the animals. Though the counselors did nothing, Mama and Papa were sure Lion would have to listen if all the animals spoke up for them.

Mama Ostrich sought out Mongoose at once. He'd helped her before, and she knew he was clever.

"How could the counselors let Lion get away?" she asked Mongoose after telling him her story. "They promised to help me get my chicks back from Lion."

"Aha, you see," said Mongoose, "it's easy for them to stand up for your rights to your face. To stand up for your rights in Lion's face is another thing."

"Well," said Mama Ostrich, "Lion may be hard-hearted, but there is a proverb: 'Infinite boiling will soften the stone.'"

"Uh-huh," said Mongoose, "but another proverb says: 'In the court where the fox is the judge, the jury foxes and the witnesses foxes, the goose doesn't stand a chance.' And you're a bird among animals."

"Oh, my!" clacked Mama Ostrich. "What can I do? I won't give up till my children are home again."

"Listen," said Mongoose. "Before you call all the animals together, dig a tunnel under the tall ant hill at the meeting ground."

"A tunnel?" asked Mama Ostrich. "What for?"

"Don't ask, just dig it," said Mongoose. "Start digging the tunnel near the assembly place. Uh-huh, go to it and do it. Dig it large enough for me, but too small for Lion! Dig, dig, dig till you've dug through to the opposite side of the ant hill. Well, all right, dig, dig, dig! When it's all dug out, don't breathe a word about the tunnel to anyone. You dig? Leave the rest to me."

Mama Ostrich dug the tunnel clear through even though she didn't know what good it would do. Then she and Papa Ostrich called all the animals to the meeting.

The animals gathered at the meeting place by the tall anthill. Chief Counselor Fox and the counselors sat facing the assembly.

"Order, order!" commanded Chief Counselor Fox. He blew his horn, "Cheerooo-cheerooo!" to quiet the animals.

"We've a serious matter to settle today," he said. "Mama and Papa Ostrich claim Lion has taken their children. Lion claims they're his. To whom do you say they belong?"

The animals looked at the chicks trembling between Lion's paws. They looked at Mama and Papa Ostrich. Uh-huh, they were not fooled.

"Ready to vote?" asked Chief Counselor Fox.

Lion stood up on two feet.

"I'll take your votes, personally, one by one," he said in a menacing tone. "You don't mind if I do, do you, chief?"

Chief Counselor Fox knew this was against the rules, but he didn't dare deny Lion's request.

Lion approached the animals one by one and took the vote. He looked straight into their eyes and asked, "Whose?"

The animals quaked and were quick to see that chicks could be cubs. In turn each agreed that the chicks were indeed Lion's children, uh-huh, uh-huh!

By the time Lion reached Mongoose, all of the animals had gone back on their promise to support Mama and

Papa Ostrich. All the votes were in favor of Lion.

"Well, Mongoose," said Lion. "Let me have your vote. That will end this meeting. I'm hungry and I want to take my children home . . . to eat."

Mama and Papa Ostrich knew just what Lion meant. They stared in alarm at Mongoose.

Mongoose looked straight back at Lion. He spoke loud and clear for all to hear.

"Lion lies!" Mongoose exclaimed. "We all have eyes. Lion may stand on two feet now, but he looks absurd. He is no bird! You all know the proverb: 'A log may lie in the water for ten years, but it will never become a crocodile!' When has anyone ever heard that fur can beget feathers? Uh-uh! The chicks are Ostriches!"

Lion stood stock still. He was stunned for the moment.
And that moment was all that Mongoose needed. He
leaped for the tunnel and escaped down the hole.

Lion came to just in time to see Mongoose flee down the
hole. Lion chased after him and dived for the hole. Pow!
He fell back and rolled over. Lion roared in anger and
tried again, but he was too large to fit through.

The meeting broke up, and the animals scattered. As they ran, they chanted:

> *"Fur beget feathers, fur beget feathers,*
> *No one's ever seen fur beget feathers."*

Mama and Papa Ostrich quickly untied their chicks and the eight Ostriches sprinted all the way home.

Lion pounced back and forth before the hole. He pawed and clawed at the entrance.

"Come out, come out!" he roared. "I'll give you 'fur beget feathers'!"

Mongoose didn't hear a word of Lion's fuss over fur and feathers. He had sped right out the other end of the tunnel and kept going.

"I know you're in there," Lion called. "You've got to come out this way, and I won't budge from here until you do. You sly Mongoose. Dog knows your name!"

Insults didn't bring Mongoose out either. He was now safe at home.

Lion finally tired of the roaring, pouncing and clawing. He crouched down on the ground before the hole and waited for Mongoose to come out.

Hours passed. Lion still sat there, too stubborn to move.

Lion grew hungrier and hungrier . . .

"I'll eat Mongoose when I catch him."

. . . and weaker and weaker . . .

"He won't give me the slip!"

. . . and fainter and thinner . . .

"Where's my Mongoose dinner?"

. . . till at last, hush, he wasted away.

Then Mama and Papa Ostrich stretched and strutted freely with their chicks.

Mama Ostrich said, "I've got a present of mangoes for Mongoose."

"Oh, mangoes for Mongoose! Mangoes for Mongoose," the six chicks cried.

Mama Ostrich and her chicks went to visit Mongoose to thank him. Mongoose came out to meet them.

The six chicks cheeped:

"Fur beget feathers, fur beget feathers,
No one's ever seen fur beget feathers."

They danced around Mongoose, singing their song, and Mama Ostrich handed Mongoose two large, juicy mangoes.

Clap for Ostrich, Mongoose, too.
Stamp for Lion. Shoo! Shoo!

THE SON OF THE WIND

Mother Wind and her son lived in a round hut on a hill. The son of the wind had no playmates. He often sat alone and looked out of the window.

When the winds blew gently, the springbok grazed on the slopes of the nearby hills. When storm winds blew, the springbok sheltered in the lee of the distant hill.

The son of the wind would look out of his window when the wind was mild and watch the wandering springbok on the slopes. He whistled softly as he watched, sweetly and softly to soothe the longing of his secret wish.

One day, the son of the wind looked out and saw a boy coming up the hill. Whooree! He had whistled his secret wish so sweetly, it had sprung to life.

The son of the wind took up his ball. He blew open the door of the hut, whoosh! and rushed out to play.

"O Nakati!" he called. "There it goes!" And he rolled the ball to the boy.

Nakati was surprised to hear his name called by a stranger.

"Who is this?" he wondered as he caught the ball. "How is it that he knows my name? I do not know his."

"O friend," Nakati called. "There it goes!" And he rolled the ball back.

Nakati did not know that the stranger was the son of the wind. Wind blows everywhere, past huts and heights, through hollows. Wind whispers its wishes wherever it blows. A child somewhere, unawares, hears the wind's wish and follows.

Wherever wind goes, wind listens. What wind hears,

wind remembers. Wind carries our secrets. Wind knows
our names.

"O Nakati! There it goes!" cried the son of the wind.

"O friend! There it goes!" cried Nakati.

They laughed and clapped as they rolled the ball between them. Back and forth the ball rolled to the calls of
"O Nakati! There it goes! O friend! There it goes!" Up
and down the slope the ball rolled till Mother Wind came
out and called her son.

Nakati listened, hoping to hear his friend's name. He
heard only sounds like the noise of the wind.

"O Nakati! When will you come to roll the ball with me again?"

"I will come again tomorrow and roll the ball with you then."

The son of the wind whistled his delight and waved good-bye to Nakati. He ran to his mother and held her hand as they walked up the hill. Then whoosh! They blew open the door of their hut and disappeared inside.

Nakati turned and ran toward home. He could hardly wait to ask his mother about the boy on the hill. She knew everyone who lived in these hills. He startled a springbok as he ran along, but he did not even notice.

"Mother! Mother!" he cried as he ran past his father into the hut. "Tell me my friend's name!"

Nakati's mother caught her son as he ran into her arms.

"First quiet down and catch your breath," she said. "Now tell me, what friend are you talking about?"

"The boy who lives on the hill," said Nakati. "He calls my name when he rolls the ball to me. He says, 'O Nakati! There it goes!' and I can only say, 'O friend! There it goes!' I would like to call his name when I roll the ball to him, just as he calls mine."

"I cannot tell you his name now, Nakati," his mother said. "You must wait until your father has finished building the windshelter for our hut. Then I will tell you his name."

Each day Nakati went to the hill and rolled the ball with his playmate. The son of the wind would call "O Nakati! There it goes!" as he rolled the ball, but Nakati could only reply, "O friend! There it goes!" as he rolled the ball in return.

Whenever Mother Wind called her son, Nakati listened to hear his name. He heard only wind sounds like "whooree" and "goowow."

"Why is it that every time I listen for my friend's name, I hear only the sound of the wind?" he wondered. Yet even though he listened carefully to Mother Wind's voice, the noise of the wind was all he heard.

Nakati helped his father so that the surrounding screen of bushes sheltering the hut would be finished faster.

"When the shelter is finished," his father said, "we will go and catch a springbok together. The air is calm and they still feed in our hills."

Finally there was little work left to do for the shelter.

"O Mother!" Nakati exclaimed. "Father's work is almost finished. Tell me now my friend's name!"

"I will tell you his name, Nakati," his mother said. "But first you must promise to keep it as a secret, you must keep it to yourself. When you roll the ball back and forth with the boy on the hill, do not say the name I will tell you until you see your father sitting down. Then you will know that the shelter is finished. Remember, do not say the name until then. You must keep it as a secret. You must keep it to yourself."

"I will wait," said Nakati. "I will keep the name a secret until I see Father sitting down. Now tell me his name."

"Your playmate is the son of the wind," said his mother. "When you say his name, it may startle him and cause him to fall. If he falls, the winds will begin to blow. So when you say his name, you must run home to the shelter of the hut as fast as you can, for he could blow you away."

"I will run, Mother. I will run faster than the wind. Tell me, please tell me! What is his name?"

"Listen carefully, my son," said his mother. "His name is Whooree-kuan-kuan. It is Gwow-gwowbootish. He is Whooree-kuan-kuan Gwow-gwowbootish."

Nakati tapped his forehead in surprise.

"Whooree-kuan-kuan Gwow-gwowbootish," he repeated. "Why, I've known it all along. I heard it everytime his mother called, but I thought it was just the sound of the wind blowing. So it was Mother Wind who called!"

Nakati snapped his fingers and spun round and round like a whirlwind.

"So that is the secret: The sound of the wind blowing is the son of the wind's name! Whooree-kuan-kuan Gwowgwowbootish."

Now Nakati knew the secret of his friend's name. He ran off to play with him.

The son of the wind saw Nakati coming. Whoosh! He blew open the door and ran out with the ball.

"O Nakati! There it goes!" cried the son of the wind. He rolled the ball as Nakati ran up the hill.

Nakati caught the ball. He remembered his promise to his mother. He looked across the field to his hut. His father had just come out to finish work on the shelter.

"O friend! There it goes!" Nakati called as he rolled the ball back.

The ball rolled back and forth between the boys. Each time Nakati looked to his home, he saw his father at work on the shelter.

"O Nakati! There it goes!"

Nakati held the ball a moment and looked to his father.

He rolled the ball back, saying, "O friend! There it goes!" for his father still had not finished work on the shelter.

Just as Nakati felt he could no longer hold the secret of his friend's name, he saw his father sit down by the door of the hut. At last his father had finished work on the shelter.

Nakati caught the ball as it came to him. Then rolling it back to the son of the wind he called:

"O Whooree-kuan-kuan! There it goes! Gwow-gwowbootish! There it goes! Whooree-kuan-kuan Gwow-gwowbootish! There it goes!"

The son of the wind looked up in surprise to hear his name called by his friend. He began to rock back and forth on his feet. Nakati did not wait for the ball to reach his playmate. Remembering his mother's warning, he turned and ran.

The ball hit the son of the wind's knees and rolled forward. As he rocked and reached for the ball, he lost his balance and fell sprawling in a hollow of the ground. There he lay, pulling at the tall grass and kicking violently.

Nakati looked back as he ran and saw that his friend had fallen. As the son of the wind rolled and tossed on the ground, the winds began to stir.

Whooree-kuan-kuan Gwow-gwowbootish bent his knees, and a snapping sound shivered the air. The winds swirled. Whooree-kuan-kuan caught the winds and spun them into a great ball.

"O Nakati! There it goes!" he called, and he flung the wind-ball after his fleeing friend.

The wind-ball rolled down the hill and bounced after Nakati. Nakati knew he could not hold back the wind-ball,

he could not roll the wind-ball back to Whooree-kuan-kuan. He felt the ball of wind at his back, Gwow-gwowbootish!

Now Nakati really ran. He ran faster than the wind, Whooree-kuan-kuan Gwow-gwowbootish! He ran into his hut and slammed the door.

The ball of wind hurled itself against the door and twirled round and round the hut, but it could not get in.

Whooree-kuan-kuan Gwow-gwowbootish rolled about where he had fallen, enjoying the strength that came to him from lying down outdoors. As he rolled on his back, kicking his feet, the storm winds increased. He bent his knees, and noises rent the air.

The winds swept along, howling and uprooting bushes, overturning weak shelters, shaking huts. Dust filled the air.

Mother Wind heard the commotion and knew that her son had fallen. She blew open the door whoosh! and rushed out of the hut calling:

"Whooree-kuan-kuan Gwow-gwowbootish! Get up! Get up!"

The son of the wind lay swirling in the whirling dust. He shouted for joy, whooree! Whooree! He didn't hear his mother. He bent one knee, the winds screeched. He cracked both knees, the winds screamed.

Whooree-kuan-kuan's mother ran up to him. She grasped him firmly and set him on his feet.

While the son of the wind lay on the ground, strong winds had blown up a storm and caused the dust to rise. Now that the son of the wind stood on his feet, the winds died down and the dust settled.

That is why the Bushmen say that when the wind stands up, the wind is still, so still it seems to be lying down, asleep. It is then that the wind blows gently.

But when the wind lies down, it is then that it seems to be standing up, awake. It is then that the wind blows violently.

While the storm winds raged, Nakati and his parents were safe and sheltered within their hut.

Nakati's father said, "Our shelter is sturdy, still I wish the wind would soon blow gently for us. The strong winds have driven the springbok away. They have gone beyond the distant hill to drink of the river yonder that flows behind that hill. If the wind stands up and we go as quietly as the wind, we may slip down to the river and catch a springbok there, before the setting of the sun."

When all was still, Nakati stepped outdoors. He looked to the distant hill of which his father had spoken. The springbok would be there, behind that hill.

Then he looked up to the hill where he had rolled the ball with the son of the wind. He whispered the name to himself, "Whooree-kuan-kuan Gwow-gwowbootish.

"Ah," Nakati said. "Aha, I see. You may walk with the

wind, you may talk with the wind, you may run and play whatever games you wish with the wind. But when the wind calls your name, you must not call the wind's name. Keep this name secret.

"It is Whooree-kuan-kuan. It is Gwow-gwowbootish! Whooree-kuan-kuan Gwow-gwowbootish!"

JACKAL'S FAVORITE GAME

Children, let me tell you 'bout Jackal and Hare.
Said, "Listen while I tell a tale of Jackal and Hare.
Jackal played at friendship,
Said, 'Playing's all I care'!"

Jackal played at friendship with Hare.

Jackal never cared at all how Hare felt, uh-uh! Jackal laughed his sad Jackal laugh and cared about nothing but playing games. He had the bad habit of tackling and tickling Hare to force him to play. So whenever Jackal saw Hare coming, Jackal put him down. Uh-huh, Jackal tackled Hare to the ground.

"La-boohoo-laha," laughed Jackal. "Playing's all I care!"

"Let go!" gasped Hare as Jackal tackled him to the prickly grass.

Jackal didn't listen to Hare's cry, uh-uh! Jackal didn't care. He only played at friendship, said "Playing's all I care." Then Jackal tickled Hare as he rolled him in the prickly grass.

"Let me hee-haw up!" giggled Hare as Jackal tickled. "Stop tickling me, hee-hee!"

"La-boohoo-laha!" laughed Jackal. "La-boohoo-laha!"

Every time they met, to get the games started, Jackal tackled and tickled Hare. He never let Hare up until he agreed to play hide-and-seek. That was Jackal's favorite game and he always cried out, "Me first! Me first! You're it!"

One day Hare was out, playing all by himself. He was having a good time too, doing the Hare-Hop and singing:

> *"I jump high, jump higher,*
> *Get ready, jump steady,*
> *To the sky, yeah!"*

"La-boohoo-laha, la-boohoo-laha."

"Uh-huh," said Hare. "That's Jackal's laugh. I'd better hide from that tickle-tackler."

Hare ducked behind a tree.

"Come out, come out, wherever you are!" cried Jackal. "I saw you jumping."

Hare didn't budge. He hummed to himself:

> *"Some friends are true friends,*
> *Some are makes-you-blue friends,*
> *You can tell by what they do*
> *Who is true, who makes you blue.*
> *And Jackal makes me blue."*

"La-boohoo-laha, I know you're hiding," said Jackal. "Hide-and-seek is my favorite game and playing's all I care."

"Uh-huh!" said Hare. "I won't play if you tackle and tickle me."

"I won't tickle or tackle," said Jackal, "but you know hide-and-seek is my game. Me first! Me first!"

Hare stepped out of hiding and asked, "How come you always go first?"

Jackal clapped his paws, clicked his claws, snapped his jaws and said:

> *"Because I'm bigger than you,*
> *Because I'm faster, too.*
> *Because I'm tough as can be,*
> *So don't you 'How come' me!"*

Jackal's reasons didn't seem fair at all to Hare, but he didn't dare go on about it, uh-uh! Jackal went first.

Jackal spun Hare around three times.

"Now, lean against the tree and count out loud," Jackal said. "Close your eyes. No peeking!"

Hare closed his eyes and chanted:

> *"Cabbages, peppers, carrots and peas,*
> *Count them by ones, by twos, by threes.*
> *I'll find you first, then I'll plant these,*
> *Cabbages, peppers, carrots and peas."*

While Hare counted, Jackal skipped off and hid in a clump of bushes. He crouched low and covered himself with twigs and leaves. Jackal was sure that Hare would never find him in his bush disguise. He didn't notice that his tail stuck out. It switched back and forth as he sang:

"I cover myself with leaves.
I close my eyes.
You'll never, ever find me
Till I yell, 'Surprise!'"

Hare looked here. Hare looked there. So far, no Jackal anywhere. Hare put his hands on his hips and hopped to the bushes. He was about to hop on when he saw a tail switch.

"Uh-huh!" said Hare. "I never saw a tail-wagging bush before."

Hare walked up to the bush and called, "Come out! Come out, wherever you are. A telltale tail's told me you're in there."

Jackal didn't budge, but his tail switched on.

Hare called again, "Come out, come out wherever you are. I spy Jackal!"

Hare stamped on Jackal's tail.

"Yow!" yelled Jackal. He jumped up and the leaves and twigs fell off of him.

"Surprise! You thought I was a bush, eh! You didn't
see me. I go again."

"Uh-uh!" said Hare. "I go now. I knew you were there.
Your tail may be bushy, but bushes don't wag tails."

Jackal brushed that off.

"I said, 'I go again!'" Jackal insisted. "Remember:

> *I'm bigger than you.*
> *I'm faster, too.*
> *I'm tough as can be,*
> *So don't you 'I go' me!"*

47

Jackal reached out, snatched Hare and spun him around three times.

"Now, count, and don't say you won't," Jackal ordered.

"Not fair," Hare murmured to himself. He didn't like being cheated out of his turn. He closed his eyes and chanted softly, so softly he could hardly be heard:

"Cabbages, peppers, carrots, peas.
Count by ones, by twos, by threes.
I'll find you, then I'll plant these:
Cabbages, peppers, carrots and peas."

Jackal scampered off to a grove of trees. He broke off some branches, then he took a vine and tied the branches around his waist.

"La-boohoo-laha," laughed Jackal. "Hiding's the best part of hide-and-seek. Now, I'm a tree. If I close my eyes, Hare won't see me."

Jackal stood up straight and still. He tucked his tail in this time, then he closed his eyes.

Hare opened his eyes. He didn't see Jackal by the home base.

"Ready or not, here I come!" Hare called.

First Hare hopped to the bush where Jackal had crouched before. He beat about the bush. No Jackal there. Hare searched the high grasses and looked behind some stones. No traces of Jackal in either of those places.

Hare ran to the grove of trees. He saw a strange sight. A tree with two legs.

"Uh-huh," said Hare:

"Your eyes are closed,
But I can see.
I spy Jackal,
One, two, three!"

Hare poked Jackal in the ribs, jaa!

"Ow!" Jackal cried. He dropped his arms and the branches. "My eyes were closed. I looked like a tree. I didn't see you. How did you see me?"

"I kept my eyes open," said Hare. "You close yours now. It's my turn. You're it."

Jackal had taken two turns and he was tempted to take three, but he relented and let Hare take a turn, too.

Now it was Hare's turn to spin Jackal around three times and to tell him, "Count out loud, I want to hear you! And close your eyes. No peeking!"

Jackal closed his eyes and leaned against a tree. He'd rather hide than seek any day. But he'd find Hare and then he'd go again, uh-huh! His count was a blues chant:

> *Okra, cassava, coconuts and corn.*
> *Said, okra, cassava, coconuts, corn.*
> *I'll count them till I find you*
> *If it takes me all day long."*

As soon as Jackal began his chant, Hare hopped off to find a good hiding place. Bippity-bop-bop, he hopped, bippity-bop-bop. He looked back to see if Jackal was peeking. Paa-lam! Hare tripped over a tree root and fell into a hole. The hole was deep enough to keep Hare well hidden from sight.

"Eh, eh!" said Hare. "What luck! I couldn't have chosen a better hiding place."

Hare made himself at home in the hole. He leaned back and stared up at the tree branches and the sky. He enjoyed watching the butterflies and birds that flew by while he waited.

Jackal finished his hide-and-seek count and set out to find Hare. He poked about in a clump of bushes and called, "Come out, come out wherever you are!"

Hare heard the loud call from wherever Jackal looked. He didn't plan to come out of his hiding hole.

Jackal came closer. Hare didn't move or make a sound. He opened his eyes wide and looked up.

Jackal saw the holes by the tree roots and he began to look into them.

Hare heard Jackal's steps coming closer and closer. He knew he would soon be discovered, but Hare was a good hide-and-seek player. He wouldn't give up until he'd been caught.

"I see you. I see you!" Jackal cried each time he looked into a dark hole. But he hadn't seen Hare yet.

> *"You may have seen a spider,*
> *You may have seen a bee,*
> *You may have seen a cricket,*
> *But you haven't seen me."*

Just then Jackal came to the hole in which Hare was hiding. Jackal looked straight into two large eyes that stared up at him out of the dark. Hare knew he'd been caught.

"Aie yaie! Aie yaie!" yelled Jackal.

He tumbled over backwards and almost caught his foot in a hole. He got to his feet and fled.

"Eh, eh!" said Hare. "What is this? Jackal found me, yet he's running away. That's no way to play hide-and-seek."

"Aie yaie! Aie yaie!" Jackal cried as he ran. "I have seen the Big-Eyed Monster. The Big-Eyed Monster is after me!"

Hare hopped out of his hole and heard Jackal's cry.

"So that's why he fled. He thinks I'm a big-eyed monster."

Hare laughed and took off after Jackal, bippity-bop-bop, bippity-bop-hop.

"Here comes the Big-Eyed Monster," Hare called. "Here comes Hare, the Big-Eyed Monster!"

"Aie yaie! Aie yaie!" Jackal wailed. "Only a monster has eyes like that! Its head must be huge. It's body, big and brutal, I bet!"

Jackal was so frightened that he didn't look where he was running. His feet caught in a vine and tripped him up. Down he went, flam!

Jackal lay there crying and panting and kicking. He couldn't untangle the vine from his feet. He closed his eyes in fright.

"The Big-Eyed Monster will get me," he cried. "La-boohoo, la-boohoo."

Hare caught up with Jackal and loosened the vine from around his feet. Jackal kept his eyes shut.

"O Big-Eyed Monster," he cried. "La-boohoo, la-boohoo! I'll do whatever you ask. Don't eat me!"

Hare sang:

> *"Because I'm bigger than you,*
> *Because I'm faster, too,*
> *Because I'm tough as can be,*
> *So don't you 'Don't eat me!'"*

Jackal opened his eyes.

"La-boohoo-lala, Brother Hare!!" Jackal cried, "Save me! This hide-and-seek game is for real. The Big-Eyed Monster is after me."

"Don't be silly," said Hare. "Look at me!"

Hare shaded his face and opened his eyes wide.

"You, Brother Hare!" Jackal exclaimed. "You're the Big-Eyed Monster!"

"Uh-huh," said Hare. "You found me, but then you ran away bawling. That's no way to play hide-and-seek."

"You scared me," said Jackal. "You shouldn't hide in dark holes and open your eyes so big and wide, not when we play hide-and-seek. Uh-uh! That's my favorite game. Promise not to do it anymore."

"You said you'd do whatever I ask when I loosened the vine from your feet," said Hare. "Promise not to tackle and tickle me anymore."

Jackal and Hare exchanged promises right then and there, and they kept them. Uh-huh, they did. Jackal stopped playing friendship with Hare and became a true friend.

After that, when Jackal and Hare played games, Jackal often said: "You first, Brother Hare. You first."

Now that's true friendship, isn't it? Uh-huh!
And playing's all I care!

THE FOOLISH BOY

There was once a bean farmer and he had a good wife. They lived together in a thatched-roof hut. They hoped for children, but as yet they had none. Still, they had each other and that made them happy.

60

On farming days, they rose early and after breakfast they walked over the hill to work in their bean field.

"Hot beans and butter!" sang the farmer as he dug into the earth.

"Come for your supper!" sang his wife as she hoed a row beside him.

They sang as they worked because farming the land was their life and they enjoyed life. Towards sunset, they returned to their hut. For supper they ate hot beans and butter with the vegetables they grew in the little garden around their hut. They didn't have meat to eat but they didn't complain. For more than meat, they longed for a child.

The years passed and their prayers for a child went unanswered. God seemed not to hear.

One day the wife thought, "Perhaps our prayers get caught up in the thatch on the roof of the hut and never get higher. Tonight I'll pray outdoors."

That night, after her husband fell asleep, the wife got up quietly. She went outdoors and prayed, "Dear God, please send me a child, even if it be a foolish one."

Well all right! God heard that prayer. He sent her a son, a simpleton.

The farmer and his wife were overjoyed to have a child. They loved their son and named him Jumoke.

The mother carried her son on her back wherever she

went until Jumoke learned to walk. Then he followed behind his parents at work in the beanfield. One day as they
planted a row of bean seeds in the earth, Jumoke picked
up the seeds and put them in his little calabash.

A villager was passing by and called out to the parents,
"See what your foolish boy is doing?"

The parents turned and saw Jumoke with his calabash full of the beans they had just planted.

They didn't get excited.
They didn't get upset.
They didn't howl or holler
And they didn't throw a fit.

Instead, they taught him how to plant the seeds.

But the name Foolish Boy stuck.

Years passed, and as the boy grew, so did the stories of his foolish ways. Finally everyone in the village called him Foolish Boy.

But his parents called him by his proper name and said, "His foolishness will make him wise. He'll surprise you one day."

Jumoke's mother was well known in the village for the delicious bean pies she baked. On big market days, she balanced a tray of bean pies on her head and set out for the market. Little Jumoke followed behind with a tray of mud pies on his head.

When they arrived in the marketplace, Jumoke set his tray of mud pies down beside his mother's tray of bean pies. The villagers bought his mother's pies quickly. She hardly had to cry out.

Jumoke cried out to all who came near or passed by, "Buy my dry mud pies!"

The villagers laughed.

"What a foolish boy Foolish Boy is!" they said to his mother.

She didn't get excited.
She didn't get upset.
She didn't howl or holler
And she didn't throw a fit.

Instead, she hugged him and said, "Don't all children say and do foolish things?"

Jumoke grew to be a fine youth. He no longer tried to sell mud pies in the market. He helped his mother carry her tray of bean pies. He'd learned many things, but the villagers still called him Foolish Boy.

One day Jumoke's parents left him to take care of the hut while they went to work in the bean field.

"Jumoke," his mother said, "cook a bean dinner for us to eat tonight."

That afternoon Jumoke put a pot filled with water on the fire. When the water boiled, he dropped in a bean and stirred.

"Don't stick to the bottom!" he said as he whipped up the bean. "Swim on top!"

When his parents returned from work, they asked:

"Is the bean dinner cooked?"

"It's in the pot," said Jumoke.

They looked in the pot. Jumoke's father shook his head and said, "A man must resign himself to what God has given him." His mother sighed.

But they didn't get excited.
They didn't get upset.
They didn't howl or holler
And they didn't throw a fit.

Instead his mother taught Jumoke how to cook a bean dinner. Then she taught her son different ways of preparing beans and how to make bean pies. She knew that although Jumoke did foolish things, he learned from his foolish ways.

One day Spider Ananse was out walking when he smelled beans cooking.

"Mmm-yum, beans," Spider said. "Smells good all right! Reminds me that my wife is cooking beans for supper tonight. Wish I had some meat to eat with those beans."

Spider followed his nose to Jumoke's hut. He saw several gazelles nibbling the vegetables in the garden around the hut.

"Oh neat! Meat!" Spider cried. "If only I had my traps with me!"

Just then Jumoke jumped out of the door and chased
after the gazelles. He tried to catch one, but they all escaped.

"Hello, Foolish Boy," said Spider Ananse. "Do the
gazelles often get into your vegetable garden?"

"No," said Jumoke. "They found our garden yesterday
and they've come back today. I chase them, but I haven't
caught one yet."

"Well, Foolish Boy," said Spider, "how would you like
to eat gazelle meat with your beans tonight?"

Jumoke stamped his feet and clapped his hands.

"Well," said Spider Ananse, "I'll bring my traps, and we'll catch them. Cook up a large pot of beans for bait. I'll be right back."

Now Spider Ananse loved to play tricks on everyone. He was so quick and clever that no one managed to trick him.

Spider Ananse had never bothered to trick Foolish Boy. He had even told his wife that Foolish Boy would be so easy to trick it wouldn't be fun. But for good gazelle meat, Spider was ready to trick anyone.

"Foolish Boy will get to see good gazelle meat all right," said Spider, laughing as he ran home. "But he won't get to eat good gazelle meat tonight. I'll beat him out of his share of the treat. Too bad Foolish Boy is going to be so easy to cheat."

Spider soon returned, riding his donkey. He sat on a large, leather bag. The traps were strapped on the donkey's back.

As soon as the beans were cooked, Jumoke helped Spider set the traps with the bean-bait. Then they hid in the hut and waited.

Soon some gazelles smelled the beans and returned to the hut. They passed up the vegetables for the bean-bait and suddenly, wham! WHAM! the traps snapped shut. Two gazelles were caught and killed. The others fled.

Spider and Jumoke ran out of hiding. They opened the traps. Jumoke watched as Spider skinned the two gazelles.

"Bring out two large baskets, Foolish Boy," Spider said. "We'll separate the good meat, swell! from the poor meat, thud!"

Jumoke brought the baskets and set them down beside Spider.

"The good meat, swell! goes into the basket on the right," said Spider. "The poor meat, thud! goes into the basket on the left."

Spider Ananse cut up the meat. Jumoke placed the meat in the baskets and sang:

> *"Good meat, swell! basket on the right*
> *Poor meat, thud! basket on the left."*

All the while that Spider cut the meat, he kept an eye on Jumoke to be sure he didn't mix up the baskets. At last the cutting and the separation was done.

"Tell me now, Foolish Boy," Spider asked, "whose traps caught the gazelles?"

"Yours, Spider," Jumoke answered. "Now tell me, Spider, whose bean-bait caught the gazelles?"

"Don't be foolish, Foolish Boy!" said Spider. "What're your beans worth beside my traps? The good meat, swell! is my share. The poor meat, thud! is your share."

"Thud!" cried Jumoke. "Thud! That's no fair share!"

But Spider didn't care about being fair when he could get away with such a slick trick.

"Go and drive my donkey here, Foolish Boy, while I empty the good meat, swell! into my bag. And be quick about it!"

Jumoke brooded on Spider's mean trick as he went in

search of the donkey. He mumbled and grumbled till he found the donkey. Suddenly Jumoke smiled. He had an idea. He drove the donkey deep into the bush and returned empty-handed.

"Where is my donkey, Foolish Boy?" Spider demanded.

"She ran off into the bush before I could catch her," Jumoke answered.

"Fool, you fool Foolish Boy!" cried Spider. "You let my donkey get away. Here, finish filling my bag with the good meat, swell! I will go and get the donkey myself. She will come if I call."

Jumoke waited until Spider was well out of sight. Then quickly he took Spider's bag of good meat, swell! and emptied it into the corn bin in the hut.

Then Jumoke tipped the poor meat, thud! into Spider's bag. He put two good pieces of meat, swell! at the top of the bag and tied it up.

Spider Ananse's donkey had circled back when Spider called. She stood at the side of the hut and watched as Jumoke filled Spider's bag with the bones and scraps. Spider caught up with his donkey just as Jumoke finished tying up the bag.

"You see, Foolish Boy, I told you she'd come if I called," Spider said. "Have you finished packing my bag?"

"Oh, yes," said Jumoke. "And it's heavy. Here, let me help you lift it onto your donkey."

Jumoke steadied the heavy bag and the traps while Spider strapped them on the donkey's back.

Spider laughed as he headed for home, thinking he would have one big surprise for his wife that night.

"Enjoy your dinner, Foolish Boy!" Spider sang as he drove the donkey along:

> *"Good meat, swell! Poor meat, thud!*
> *Fooling folk is in my blood.*
> *To fool a fool may not be fair,*
> *But I should worry, I should care!"*

Spider beat out the rhythms on the poor donkey's back. A-whack! A-whack! A-whack!

"Faster! Faster!" Spider cried. "I'm getting hungry!"

The blows stung and finally the donkey could take it no longer. She sang out:

> *"Swell or thud; like it or not,*
> *It's stomach, liver and scraps you've got."*

"What are you saying?" cried Spider.

He gave the donkey a harder whack with his stick. "Sing rather:

> *"Even Dog and Cat will have a treat,*
> *For I took the tip-top tasty meat."*

But no matter how hard Spider hit, the donkey continued to sing:

> *"Cat and Dog will have a treat,*
> *They'll get the tip-top tasty meat.*
> *But swell or thud, like it or not,*
> *It's stomach, liver and scraps you've got."*

Spider was so aggravated by these words that he beat the donkey all the way home.

When Jumoke's parents returned from work in their
bean field, they entered the hut and smelled the meaty
aroma coming from the hot beans pot.

"Hot beans and butter," sang Jumoke as they looked in
the pot.

"And meat for our supper!" his mother exclaimed.

"Couldn't be better," his father said.

"There's meat for days to come, too," said Jumoke. He led his parents to the corn bin.

"Where did you get all this good meat?" his parents asked.

Jumoke danced and sang:

> *"You didn't get excited.*
> *You didn't get upset.*
> *You didn't howl or holler*
> *And you didn't throw a fit.*

And now I've done something good."

Then Jumoke told his parents the story of how Spider Ananse had tried to trick him, and how he had turned the trick on Spider.

"Why, good meat, swell! Poor meat, thud!" sang the parents. "You sure tricked that trickster Spider. No one has ever done that before."

"No more talk now," said Jumoke, laughing. "Come for your supper."

But first his mother and father hugged him tight. Then they all sat down to a delicious supper of hot beans and butter and good meat, swell!

Spider Ananse reached home and called his wife:

"Koki! Hey, Koki! I've a surprise for you. Bring the large calabash that belonged to your ancestors. This is a special occasion."

Cat and Dog heard Spider and came running. Cat rubbed up against Spider's legs! Dog sat up and begged.

Spider opened the sack. He tossed one top piece of meat to Cat. He tossed another top piece of meat to Dog.

Spider's wife returned with the large calabash. She saw Cat and Dog running off with juicy morsels of meat in their mouths.

"Aha!" said Spider Ananse, laughing. "See that, eh? Tonight Dog and Cat eat good meat, swell! And so will we, Koki. So will we! Just wait till you see!"

Koki set the large calabash on the ground, and Spider poured the contents of the bag into it.

"What is this?" cried Koki. "Bones! Stomach! Scraps! Is this what you want my good calabash for—the calabash of my ancestors?"

"Oh, no! Oh, no!" cried Spider. "Poor meat, thud! How did that happen? Here, Cat! Here, Dog!"

But Cat and Dog had run off with the good meat, swell! And would not come back.

Koki picked up a leg bone, shook it at Spider and shouted, "You give Dog and Cat good meat, swell! And this is what you give me? Well, this is what I give you!"

Koki swung the leg bone, wham! and gave Spider one hard blow across his back.

The donkey sang:

"Swell or thud, like it or not.
It's stomach, liver and scraps you've got."

"Oh, donkey," Spider wailed, "you were telling the truth after all and I beat you. If only I had listened to you instead."

Spider stroked the donkey gently and said, "How I have wronged you! I promise never to beat you again. I, the **trickster, deserve** blows for letting a fool fool me. Not you! What a wicked trick he played on me!"

"You don't mean you let Foolish Boy trick you?" said Koki in surprise. "But you've always said it wasn't worth tricking Foolish Boy, it would be too easy."

"Oh, I know! Oh, oh, oh!" wailed Spider.

"A simple switch-trick like that, and you fell for it, Spider!" said Koki.

Koki was about to serve Spider another well-deserved leg bone blow, when suddenly her anger gave way. She dropped the leg bone, threw her arms around the donkey's neck and burst out laughing.

The donkey hee-hawed along with her.

"Thud!" said Spider. "Just wait till tomorrow. I'll get even with him!"

The next morning Spider Ananse set out to call on Jumoke. He was determined to even the score before the story of Foolish Boy's switch-trick made the rounds in the village.

Jumoke's parents had prepared him for Spider's return before they left for work in the fields.

When Spider arrived, there sat Jumoke at the entrance to his hut, covered from head to foot with ashes.

Spider knew this was a sign of sorrow. He couldn't imagine why Foolish Boy was in mourning, and he didn't care about it either. He had troubles enough of his own.

"Peace be upon you," said Spider Ananse.

"And upon you, peace," Jumoke replied.

Spider didn't waste a minute. He burst out crying, "You cheated me, Foolish Boy! You played a trick on me. I opened my bag of meat at home and found only poor meat, thud!"

"Oh, Spider," Jumoke cried, "don't talk to me about good meat, swell! and poor meat, thud! It's all bad meat to me now."

"How can that be? You took all the good meat, swell!" said Spider.

"Yes," said Jumoke, "but those gazelles that were caught in your traps were the Chief's gazelles. He's sent a messenger to my father. He wants to know what happened to the gazelles you caught."

"I'm not in this!" said Spider.

"The Chief wants the gazelles back, Spider, because they belong to him."

"Oh, poor Foolish Boy," said Spider. "I see you are in trouble."

"Help me, Spider," Jumoke pleaded. "Take the good meat, swell! before the Chief finds it here."

"I wouldn't touch it, Foolish Boy," said Spider. "I must go home now. Koki, my wife, is waiting for me."

Spider bent down and sprinkled more ashes on Jumoke.

"I'm sorry, but that's all I can do to help you, Foolish Boy," said Spider. "May God make it easy for you. Good-bye!"

Spider Ananse couldn't get away from there fast enough. He ran home chuckling to himself.

"Aha, aha! Foolish Boy is indeed in trouble. I was afraid for a moment that I couldn't get free of him. What a clever trickster I am!

"This is just the way I intended it to turn out!"

"Good meat, swell! Poor meat, thud!
Fooling folk is in my blood.
To fool a fool may not be fair,
But I should worry, I should care!"

But you and I know better. The villagers knew better. Even the donkey knew better.

When Spider Ananse learned that Foolish Boy had tricked him not just once, but twice, he took to his bed. He lay there for ten days and wouldn't touch meat. Then he got up, packed his goods and moved away from that village.

From the stories we've heard since then of Spider Ananse, we know that he's still busy tricking others. But ever since Foolish Boy tricked him, he's moved on whenever he's been tricked. And since that does happen sometimes, stories of Spider Ananse have spread far and wide.

Jumoke's parents loved him and had been patient with him. They had taught him to learn from his mistakes. They believed that in this way even a simpleton could become wise.

The villagers now praised the boy's wit more than they had ever laughed at his foolishness. They no longer called him Foolish Boy. They called him by his proper name, Jumoke, just as his parents always had.

And more than ever before, everyone loved the child.

Poor meat, thud! Good meat, swell!
Don't you know another story to tell?

CREDITS

LION AND THE OSTRICH CHICKS:
THE MASAI, THEIR LANGUAGE AND FOLKLORE,
    ALFRED C. HOLLIS. OXFORD: THE CLARENDON PRESS,
    1905. PAGE 198

THE SON OF THE WIND:
SPECIMENS OF BUSHMAN FOLKLORE,
    BLEEK AND LLOYD. LONDON: GEORGE ALLEN & COM-
    PANY, LTD., 1911. PAGES 100–107

JACKAL'S FAVORITE GAME:
FOLK-TALES OF ANGOLA,
    HELI CHATELAIN. BOSTON: AMERICAN FOLK-LORE
    SOCIETY MEMOIRS I, 1894. PAGE 209

THE FOOLISH BOY:
HAUSA TALES AND TRADITIONS, VOLUME I,
    TRANSLATED AND EDITED BY NEIL SKINNER, FROM
    TATSUNIYOYI NA HAUSA BY FRANK EDGAR. AF-
    RICANA PUBLISHING CORPORATION, 1969. PAGES
    14–15, 17–19